The Cat Who
His Purr

Michele Coxon

PUFFIN BOOKS

Bootle woke one morning
without his purr.
His house was quiet and empty.
"Where is my purr?" wondered Bootle,
who was normally happy and
contented.
He thought hard.
"When did I have it last?"
But like all cats he was not very good
          at remembering yesterday.

He didn't know about things like
"tomorrow," or the names of
the days of the week.
Or even that the world was round.
To him it was flat,
and today it was purrless.
The things he knew were useful, like if it
was a wet fur day or a dry fur day.
Or what time his cans were opened and
when his milk was poured.
"I will go and find my purr," decided
Bootle, and he set off.

Bootle started by looking
in the bathroom.
Drip, drip, drip, drop, went the tap.
"Is this my purr?"
No, the wet drip sound
was not his purr.
"Is my purr down here?"
No, it was not in the place where his
unfurry friends sometimes sat.

Bootle heard something that sounded like his purr.

Buzz, buzz, buzz.

"Is this my purr?"

No, it was just a fly, so he ate it.

"Where did the noise go?" wondered Bootle, licking his lips.

He went downstairs to the kitchen
where there were lots of
interesting sounds.
Humm, humm, humm.
The fridge hummed softly and it smelled
good. Bootle was a clever cat. He knew
how to open the fridge and look inside.
"Is my purr here?"
"No, not even inside the sausages,"
thought Bootle, feeling rather full.

There was a sound from
under the cupboard.
Scratch, scratch, scratch, squeak.
"That sound could be my purr."
But the *scratch, squeak* ran away from
his fine, sharp claws.

A pleasant *tick, tick, tock* came
from the clock.
"Could that be my purr?" he wondered.
Bootle climbed up, but a yellow bird
knocked him down with a loud
"Cuckoo!"
"Meow!" yelled Bootle.

In the laundry room the washing
monster made lots of loud, wet
gurgling noises.
Swish, swish, swash.
"Is my purr in the wash?"
Bootle thought a cat thought
(which isn't very long) and watched
until his whiskers felt dizzy.
"No, my purr is not there. It hates
getting wet."

In the living room the fish blew bubbles
at him from their watery world.
Bubble, bubble, bubble.
Bootle didn't like getting his paws wet
so he could not find out
if the fish had his purr.
He turned away sadly.

"My purr must be outside in the sunshine. It loves the warm sun," thought Bootle. But he had to chase away some naughty birds who were stealing his milk. *Crash!*

In the garden, a robin was banging
something on a stone.
Crack, crack, crack.
Could it be his purr?
Bootle rushed to the rescue. But it was
only an unhappy snail which crawled
away without saying thank you.
Cats appreciate good manners.
Snails are always miserable
and never smile.

Bootle went back to the house
in a down-tail mood.
Cats don't cry because that
makes them wet.
"Poor me," sighed Bootle.
He had a drink of milk, to help him
think, and licked all the chocolate off
some biscuits just for comfort.

And then he heard a sound.
Lots of sounds, coming into the house.
Voices of his two-legged,
unfurry friends.
"My openers of cans.
My pourers of cream.
My strokers of fur."
They were home and
they had found his purr.
He purred with joy.
Purr, purr, purr, purr, purr.

At last his life (which to a cat
means today) was purr-fect.
He was the most contented cat in the
whole flat garden of his world and
would be until the end of his whiskers.
And now his tale is told.

*In memory of Karen and her husband Charlie and their
children, Ben, Katy, and Becky.*

PUFFIN BOOKS
Published by the Penguin Group
Penguin Putnam Inc., 375 Hudson Street, New York,
New York 10014, U.S.A.
Penguin Books Ltd, 27 Wrights Lane, London W8 5TZ, England
Penguin Books Australia Ltd, Ringwood, Victoria, Australia
Penguin Books Canada Ltd, 10 Alcorn Avenue, Toronto, Ontario,
Canada M4V 3B2
Penguin Books (N.Z.) Ltd, 182-190 Wairau Road, Auckland 10,
New Zealand

Penguin Books Ltd, Registered Offices: Harmondsworth,
Middlesex, England

First published in the United Kingdom by Blackie Children's Books,
a division of Penguin Books Ltd, 1991
First American edition published by Peter Bedrick Books, 1992
Published in Puffin Books, 1996

5 7 9 10 8 6 4

Copyright © Michele Coxon, 1991
All rights reserved

Puffin Books ISBN 0-14-055608-7

Printed in the United States of America